Read!

Short Vowel Sounds

A Little T-Rex Book

By Jeanne Schickli & Tara Cousins

Table of Contents

Book 1: Pam – short "a"

Book 2: Ben Begs – short "e"

Book 3: Swim to Win – short "i"

Book 4: Frogs – short "o"

Book 5: My Bug Gus – short "u"

Book 1:

Pam

Pam sat on the cat.

1

The cat ran.

Pam sat on the hat.

The hat is flat.

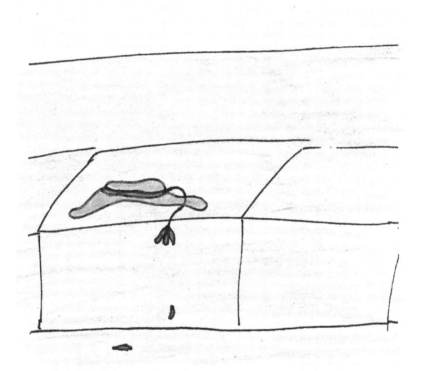

Pam has a pan of ham.

Pam has a jar of jam.

Pam has a crab...

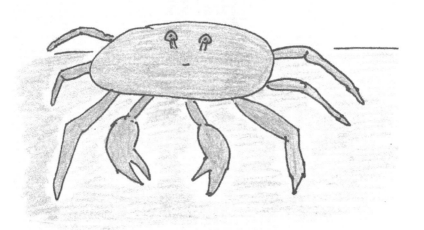

and a glass...

9

That is that.

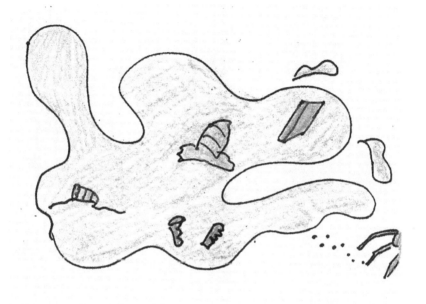

Book 2:

Ben Begs

My Dog is Ben.

1

Ben begs.

2

Ben begs for chips.

I toss Ben a chip.

Ben begs to go out.

Ben went out.

Ben begs to go in.

Ben went in.

I bend to pet Ben.

The End.

Book 3:

Swim to Win

Jim is a fish.

Jim is slim.

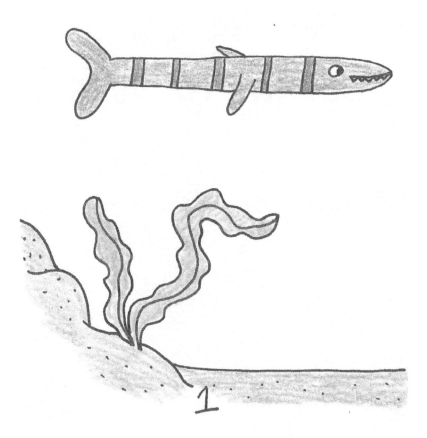

1

Kim is a fish.

Kim has a big fin.

Tim is a fish.

Tim has a small fin.

Jim swims.

Kim swims.

Tim swims.

Jim, Kim and Tim swim fast.

Jim, Kim and Tim want to win.

5

Will Kim win?

Will Jim win?

7

Will Tim win?

8

Kim wins!

Kim is first.

10

Book 4:

Frogs

Bob and Tod are frogs.

Bob hops off the log.

Tod hops off the log.

Bob and Tod hop
on and off the log.

Plop! Plop! in the bog.

Ron has a hot rod.

He likes it a lot.

Ron got Bob the frog in the bog.

Ron got Tod the frog in the bog.

Ron, Bob and Tod
in the hot rod.

They went far.

They did not stop.

Book 5:

My Bug Gus

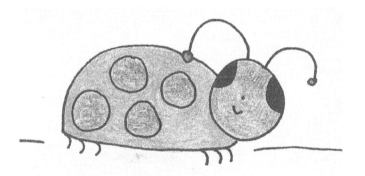

That is my bug.

I call him Gus.

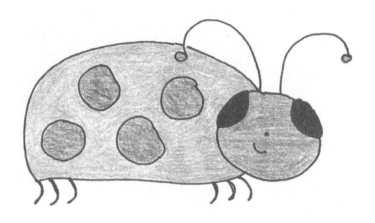

I put Gus in a box.

He got out.

I made a fuss.

I put Gus in a big
box...

...but he went up and
he got out.

I put Gus in a
big, big box.

But he went up...

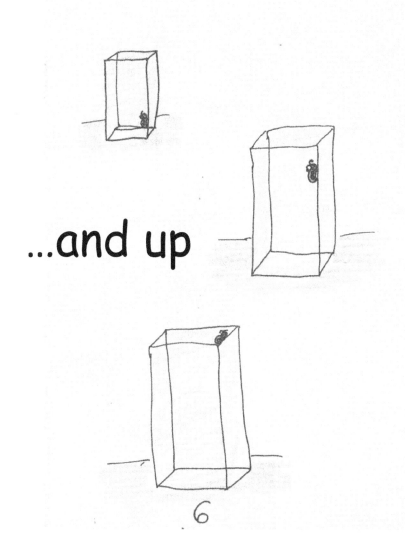

...and up

...and he got out.

7

I put grass in the
box with Gus.

But Gus got out!

9

I put Gus in my yard.
Gus dug in the grass.
Now Gus is snug as a
bug in a rug.

The End

Thanks for reading!

Visit www.amazon.com for the next two books in the **Now I Can Read!** Series:

Volume 2: Long Vowel Sounds

Volume 3: 5 Silly Stories for Early Readers

CPSIA information can be obtained
at www.ICGtesting.com
Printed in the USA
BVHW032306240920
589612BV00001B/76

9 781503 026698